The Adventures of Dusty Sourdough

by Glen Guy

THE ALASKA WILDERNESS SERIES   BOOK 2

IN THE ADVENTURE

Trail To Wrangell

Production By

Publication Consultants *Since 1978*

PUBLISHED BY

O.A.T

OLD ALASKA TODAY—WASILLA, ALASKA

ISBN 1-888125-23-3

Library of Congress Catalog Card Number: 97-69638

Copyright 2000 by Glen Guy
—First Printing 1995 —
—Second Printing 1997 —
—Third Printing 2000 —
—Fourth Printing 2005 —

This is a work of fiction, based on actual Alaska events of the 1800s. Many of the characters appearing in The Adventures of Dusty Sourdough were very real, and some of the incidents actually took place. But, the reader should be aware that, in the developing of characters and events, some fictional literary license has been employed. While some of the characters and events herein are purely the creation of the author, every effort has been made to portray them with accuracy. However, the inherent dangers of wilderness are real, sufficient unto themselves, and seldom has it been necessary to enhance their reality.

Illustrations by John Setterlund and others.

Manufactured in the United States of America.

To all Dusty's fans who like him,
feel they were born a century too late.

And to my precious grandchildren, Crystal
and Nicolas. The little ones grow up so fast.

Books by Glen Guy

A Gift for Dusty

The Trail to Wrangell

Adventure Gold

Fire!

Trail's End

≈ CHAPTER I ≈

Even though most everyone in town was saying this winter was the worst they could ever remember, Dusty couldn't have been happier. His adventures as a cowboy, calvary scout, and Indian fighter on the western frontier, never seemed to hold his interest. He was always looking for what was waiting on the other side of the hill and when arriving, whatever he was looking for wasn't to be found, so another hill beckoned him in his never ending search. Dusty didn't know at the time, but his journey north would be the end of his lifelong quest. In this land he would at last find peace and his destiny, in a settlement called Hope … On the last frontier.

The town meeting was well underway when Dusty and Shadow Spirit stepped through the door. "As we all know," George Roll, the store-keeper was saying, "this winter is a bad one. One we hope only comes along once in a lifetime. I know all of yah is runnin' short on grub, and I hav' ta tell yah the store is too. As yah can see fer yourselves, the shelves are practically empty. Johnny Dynamite[1] hasn't been able to get the Utopia up the inlet to resupply us and no one has made it over the pass since Dusty did, back before Christmas."[1, 2]

Just the mention of the narrow escape from the cave in Resurrection Pass gave Dusty a very uneasy feeling. It was the same feeling he had back in the cave, when the hair on the back of his neck stood up, warning him that a pair of unseen eyes were watching him from some-where in the blackness of his sanctuary.[3] Some-times when he and Shadow Spirit ventured into the nearby forest, to get familiar with the sur-roundings, that same feeling would come over him. Something or someone was watching him!

Dusty's attention was brought back to the meeting by the sound of V.O. Rollie's voice saying, "I reckon if I don't get me some meat and dry goods I'll hav' ta be a closen' my Grub Tent. One of us is gonna hav' ta go a huntin' … and I mean right soon. There won't be any help a comin' from Fort Resurrection.[4, 5] With all the snow we've had, there's no way a body could

get through the Pass! ... So who's it gonna be?
... Who's a-volunteerin'?"

The room became dead quiet. It was so quiet
you could hear the crackling fire in the old pot
belly stove and the steady ticking of the Regu-
lator clock hanging on the wall above the
empty drygoods' barrels. After what seemed
like an eternity, Dusty heard his own voice
saying, "Why shucks, I reckon I could give it a

try. While I was down in the Wyomin' territory a
few years ago, I worked for the railroad a-huntin'
buffalo ta feed the crew that was a-buildin' what
I called the end of a way of life."

As Dusty spoke, no one noticed the sadness that

came into his eyes. The life he once knew as a cowboy and a free spirit in the Old West, he knew, would never come again. With the railroad and the invention of barbed wire, the West changed fast and the open range would soon be no more.

When by chance, on a wet gray rainy day in a Seattle waterfront cafe, Dusty met a man named King who changed his life forever. As King told his story of gold just laying on the ground for the taking in a place called Alaska, Dusty thought his ore cart was a few shovels short of a full load. ... That is until he pulled out four pokes of gold. It goes without saying, this got Dusty's undivided attention, and King talked on and on about this place he kept calling, The Last Frontier. Without a shadow of a doubt, Dusty knew destiny was calling him to this vast wilderness of the midnight sun. ... A place called Alaska.

"Oh Dusty!" Aura Lee cried, jumping to her feet with fear in her voice. "Why should you be the one to go?" Aura Lee then turned to face the surprised town folks and asked, "What's the matter with all of you? ... How can any of you let Dusty go into the bush? He hasn't been here long enough to know how to survive a blizzard or a sudden drop in temperature. ... Someone else just has to go! Please, Pleeese don't let him go!"

Again there was nothing but silence. No one looked her in the eye, not a person spoke up to be a volunteer. She stood there not believing what was happening. Finally in an even, steady voice Aura Lee said, "You're all a bunch of cowards, and if you let Dusty go, and if something happens to him, I'll never forgive any of you!" With that said, she spun around in a flurry and stomped out of the store. Everyone looked at each other in astonishment, or should I say amazement. Until now they all thought Aura Lee was just a quiet, school teacher. Well, now they knew better.

"Now, would you ever in your born days imagine that sweet little lady havin' grit like that?" the storekeeper asked. Everyone chuckled, breaking the uneasy feeling permeating the store. The code of the West carried up to the last frontier, and part of that code was not to ask a person about his or her past, so when V.O. Rollie cleared his throat and began to speak of his past, it peaked everyone's curiosity.

"I guess before Dusty came to town I was the Cheechako[6] around here. I surely do appreciate the fact that none of yah ever asked about my past. I know yah all have often wondered why I don't wear a gun." The next words that came, from the normally jolly cafe owner, was a surprise to everyone. "First of all; I wasn't always a cook and cafe owner. Before I came to Hope I was a lawman running on fifteen years in the Arizona Territory. I was a good one too ... that is, until the day the McKinney gang came to town."

"The west bound stage had just pulled up in front of the Wells Fargo office. All of a sudden, the peaceful morning stillness was shattered by the unmistakable sound of gunfire. I was at the barber shop getting a shave. I sprang to my feet, wiped the shaving soap from my face, and out the door I went, colt in hand. A bullet smashed into the door jam above my head. Throwing myself to the ground, I fired back at one of the gang members running for his horse. That's when it happened.

"It felt as if I had been kicked in the head by a forty dollar army mule, then a searing wave of pain racked my entire body. I closed my eyes and clenched my teeth, trying to make the pain go away. When I opened them, everything started moving in slow motion. I tried to lift my colt, but my arm wouldn't respond. The gun went off, firing into the dirt.

"After that I didn't know a thing until I came to, in bed, at Millie's boarding house with Doc Barns a standin' over me. He had a real worried look on his face, and when I tried to speak I couldn't make anything come out. I must have passed out again, because the next time I regained consciousness, Millie was by my bedside, and the look of concern on her face, well it wasn't anymore encouraging than that of Doc Barns.

"I said I was thirsty and asked for a drink of water, you could see the relief flow into her face. As we talked, she filled me in on what had happened.

"The McKinney gang was robbing the Wells Fargo office of the gold shipment that arrived on the west bound stage. She said I had tried to stop them, but they out numbered me ten to one. Lead was flyin' around like a bunch of mad hornets. I was shootin' back, and holdin' my own too. I even plugged me one of those polecats, but that's when I almost went under. I got hit in the head, just above my ear, by a ricochet. Doc Barns said I had the hardest head he had ever seen."

Removing his hat, V.O. lifted his hair above his left ear and revealed an ugly two-inch scar. "It took me months before I was able to get around on my own, and at last I thought I was pert near healed. ... I was fixin' ta go back ta sheriffin' when Doc Barns came by my room and told me something that would change my life forever. He said that the dizzy spells, that came over me at unsuspectin' times, would probably always happen. In fact, he said they could get worse, and I should consider another line of work. If I should have a dizzy spell, or even pass out with my colt in hand, it could go off and shoot an innocent bystander. It would be tough to live with if it ever happened. After three days of thinkin' on it, I turned in my badge and hung up my guns—forever.

"After that I just drifted for the next two years, what happened in that time wasn't important. To make a long story short, somehow I ended up here in Hope slinging hash in my Grub Tent. ... I truly wish I could be the one to go huntin,' but I'm sad to say, I don't even own a gun any longer."

As Dusty sat there listening to V.O. lay his past bare for everyone to judge. He couldn't help wondering about all the other untold stories in the room. It took some nerve to do what V.O. had done and Dusty couldn't help but admire him.

The rest of the men came up with their own reasons for not being able to leave town. Some, like Charlie Miller,[7] were afraid of claim jumpers taking over their mines if they were gone too long. Others had pretty feeble reasons, and Dusty couldn't help wondering about their metal.

"Well, I reckon I best go clean and oil my ole Hawkens and get my gear ready. I'll be a leavin' at first light. … That is if no one else has an objection?"

With Shadow Spirit by his side, Dusty walked out the door into the cold, crisp Alaska night.

⪼ CHAPTER 2 ⪼

Aura Lee, stumbling from the store with tears flowing freely down her cheeks, was making her way back to her quarters, located in the rear of the school house. She knew she had made a fool of herself. Now the whole town knew of her feelings for Dusty.

"Oh well," she said to herself, "I hope Dusty doesn't think I'm too outspoken, and won't want anything to do with me."

As Aura Lee turned down the path leading to the school house, a noise coming from behind her caused her heart to skip a beat. Whirling around, with fear constricting her throat and a shaky voice, she managed a, "Who... who's there? I've a gun. ... I ... I know how to use it!" She stammered, looking into the darkness.

Standing as still as a statue, she could hear her own pulse beating like a drum, but to her relief she could hear nothing else.

With weak knees, Aura Lee turned and started down the path. She hadn't traveled but a few steps when she heard the noise again. As she started to turn, a crashing sound came from the dark forest. It was too late for her to do anything but brace herself, for the inevitable attack! ... ...

⚘ CHAPTER 3 ⚘

Dusty, with Shadow Spirit by his side, left the meeting at the general store, and started for One Eyed Reilly's cabin. The temperature was well below zero and the night sky was like none anywhere in the world. Dusty stood looking up in awe at the spectacular show of greens, golds, and white of the Northern Lights dancing across the black velvet sky of the Alaska night.

"It's a mighty cold night ole girl," Dusty said, turning to pat Shadow Spirit on the head, but to his surprise she was nowhere in sight. "Now where has that four legged, tail waggin' critter got to? She can disappear faster than anything I ever knowed. ... ... Shadow Spirit! ... Shadow, where in tarnation are yah?!" ... Dusty called and called, but to no avail, there wasn't even an answering bark, only the whisper of the wind in the snow-laden boughs of the surrounding forest.

"If she doesn't show up by mornin', I guess I'll just have ta leave without her." With that said, Dusty turned and continued down the path to the cabin. As he reached the door he glanced along his back trail, pulled the latch, and went inside. Dusty took down his ole caliber 54 Hawkens, cleaned and oiled it, and then got his trail-worn pack out from under his bunk.

Aura Lee was right. Dusty didn't know much about surviving in this vast wilderness. A man could freeze to death in moments if he didn't know how to stay warm, and that wasn't the worse thing that could happen to him. With as much care as possible, Dusty started carefully putting things he thought he might need into his pack.

Reaching for the shelf above the stove for coffee makin's, his hand froze in midair. … Were his ears playing a trick on him? Did he hear a scream, or was it just the wind? Dusty strained to listen for the sound he thought he had heard only moments before. … … There. There it was again!

He wasn't imagining it. Pulling on his heavy fur coat, and with his Hawkens in hand, he charged out the door and down the trail toward the sound which had interrupted his packing.

Fear struck; Aura Lee spun around, as she did, her foot slipped in the snow and down she went, on her backside, with a thud. Before she could recover her footing the menace from out of the dark forest was on top of her. At that same

moment, as a big pink tongue came across her face, she recognized her assailant, and burst into laughter with relief and joy.

"Shadow Spirit, you scared the wits out of me. ... You should be ashamed of yourself." She stood, brushing the snow off and then reaching to give the big wolf-dog a loving pat on the head.

～〜〜

"Hey!" a voice called from the dark. "There yah are, yah old scallywag." Dusty exclaimed. "I guess yah decided to go a callin' without me, Yah should be ashamed of yourself. … botherin' Miss Aura Lee that-a-way."

"Oh, she's no bother Dusty. She just gave me a fright for a moment. …"

"Well if ya'd like. … Me an' her'd be glad ta walk yah the rest of the way home?" Dusty volunteered with a shyness to his voice he hoped Aura Lee wouldn't notice.

"Why, that would be right nice … and maybe you would like to come in and sit a spell … I mean have a cup of tea … I mean coffee … I mean … Aura Lee could feel the red flush of embarrassment traveling up her neck and into her face. The harder she tried to be nonchalant, the worse it got.

Finally, Dusty chuckling to himself, seeing the predicament Aura Lee was working herself into, thankfully interrupted her by asking. "Have yah got any of that there sugar stuff? That would go right nice in a cup of coffee."

While Aura Lee got a fire going in her cook-stove and prepared the coffee, Dusty couldn't help but notice how comfortable her quarters were, and it was then, while looking about, that an unfamiliar feeling came over him.

In all his days he never thought he could be so content sitting, but to his surprise he was, and more than that, he found himself not wanting it to end. It was hard for Dusty to say good night after enjoying a sweet, hot cup of coffee ... not to mention the warmth he felt in his heart, when in the company of Aura Lee. He knew he had to finish getting ready for his adventure starting at first light, so Dusty reluctantly said goodbye and headed for the door.

"Wait!" Aura Lee said, reaching for a brightly colored woolen scarf hanging on a hook by the door. "This will remind you that you have a home cooked meal, with dried apple pie for desert, to come back too."

"Why Miss Aura Lee ... Are yah a givin' me an invite ta dinner when I get back?"

"I ... I guess I am ... Please be careful, and don't take any chances you don't have to."

～～

Starting back down the trail, with thoughts of

Aura Lee dancing in his head, Dusty didn't hear Shadow Spirit's first warning growl. The second one was much more intense and this time it got Dusty's undivided attention. Another low guttural growl came from deep within her chest as he turned in the direction the wolf-dog was looking.

Dusty brought the hammer back on his Hawkens and stood stock still. The forest was dark and ominous and when Dusty called out, there wasn't an answer. Suddenly Dusty noticed something very strange. ... Shadow Spirit was still growling and even barking toward the forest ... but her tail was wagging.

"Hey girl, what's going on here? ... Are yah givin' me a warnin', or are yah greeting a friend?" Puzzled, Dusty reached down and patted Shadow Spirit's head. It was then that he noticed the hair was standing up on the back of his neck.

"There's someone out there watching us girl, but I don't have to tell you that ... do I? Come on, who ever it is I don't think he's going to show himself. We've got more to do before we can light shuck in the morning."

After getting the rest of his things together, Dusty laid down on his bunk and quickly fell off to sleep.

Dusty didn't know what had awakened him, or even how long he had been asleep, but he knew something, or someone, had caused the hair on the back of Dusty's neck to stand up.

Laying there in the dark, ears straining for the slightest sound, Dusty remained motionless ... But for what? Sensing Shadow Spirit's movement, more than seeing it in the darkness, Dusty reached down beside his bunk and felt that the big wolf-dog was alert, and stock-still, with her ears pointed toward the door.

"What is it girl ... do yah hear somethin' out there?"

With a bark, she sprang for the door. Dusty leaped to his feet, grabbed his trousers with one hand and his Hawkens with the other.

"Hold on, hold on, let me get my pants on."

As he reached the door, the whole inside of the cabin lit up with bright lantern light. "Hey ... what's all the ruckus? Can't a feller get some shut-eye around here?" One Eyed Reilly said, as he lit a lantern and blew out the match.

Dusty was out the door following Shadow

Spirit, before One Eye could utter another word. Standing at the edge of the clearing, where the cabin was nestled, Dusty stopped to figure out which way Shadow Spirit went. He couldn't hear a thing; not even a bark or a growl from the dark forest to indicate the direction she had gone.

Standing in the subzero temperature for a moment, Dusty decided to return to the warmth of the cabin and let her chase whatever it was that had awakened them.

One Eye was up and getting the cook stove fire going when Dusty stepped through the door. "Well?" ... He asked, with a puzzled look.

Dusty explained how he had been awakened and could see or hear nothing when he went outside to investigate. One Eye just shook his head, and offered no explanation to the strange goings on. For some unknown reason he didn't want to tell Dusty the same thing had happened to him in the past. ... He too had felt the presence of some unseen person—more than once!

≋ CHAPTER 4 ≋

After a huge breakfast of sourdough flapjacks, birch syrup, bacon and plenty of hot coffee, Dusty put his gear on, said his goodbye and stepped into the early morning light. He headed through town and picked up a trail that went west along the inlet toward Chickaloon Bay.

He hadn't gone far when the familiar sound of Shadow Spirit's bark came to his ears. Turning, he saw her charging up his back trail as fast as her legs could carry her. When she reached him, he bent down and stroked her big head saying, "Hey! what's the rush?" I knew you'd catch up ta me sooner or later. Where yah been? … I sure wish yah could talk. I bet the conversation would be right interestin'."

Of course she couldn't speak, but if she could,

it would have shocked him to know what she had found in the woods. Unfortunately, all she could do was show her happiness by her body movements and a forever wagging tail.

"Let's get on down the trail and see about huntin' up some meat!"

The trail was well marked and easy to follow, so Dusty and Shadow Spirit made good time. As the sun broke over the snow-covered mountains to the east, the inlet waters shimmered like liquid gold in the breaking light of a jeweled morning. Breakup was underway and it wouldn't be long before the ice left the valleys. Even now Dusty could feel the warmth of the sun on the side of his face as he came to the edge of a clearing. There were a heap of tracks in the clearing, and by their size and shape, Dusty knew a moose had passed this way ... and not long ago.

Speaking to Shadow Spirit in a hushed tone Dusty said, "it looks like we're in luck. These here tracks are fresh, so we'll need to move real careful like ... yah understand?"

He was always amazed how well she understood his every word. As he started tracking the moose across the clearing, Shadow Spirit, close on his heels, fell in behind at full alert. The trail led up and away from the inlet and into the trees. At first the going wasn't bad, but after a short distance the climb got steeper, and Dusty found himself stopping more frequently to rest. It was during one of these rest periods that he noticed the sun had given way to menacing gray clouds.

The wind picked up and carried with it, a message that mother nature wasn't ready to give up her wintery, icy grip—not yet! More than once Dusty heard people say how unpredictable the weather was here in this far north land, and he was about to find out just how harsh the sudden changes could be.

It wasn't long before snow started falling. It always astounded Dusty how still and beautiful it became during a gentle snow fall, and he was hoping that this was all it was going to be ... a gentle snow fall. The moose tracks were getting more arduous to follow and the snow was coming down harder when Dusty caught a glimpse of something moving through the trees. Dropping to one knee and bringing his Hawkens up, he waited, hoping that at last, he had caught up to the moose he had tracked most of the day. In that moment of thought, out it stepped, the biggest moose he had ever seen.

When it stepped into the middle of the trail,

Dusty's reflexes must have taken over, because he couldn't even remember pulling back the hammer on his Hawkens. All he heard was the thunderous roar of it going off and then the huge animal going down. Dusty reloaded his rifle, and with the utmost caution, approached the animal that would put meat on the dinner tables of Hope. The moose was huge. Close up it looked as big, or bigger, than any animal Dusty had ever taken for food.

"Well Lord ... I sure do thank yah for this magnificent creature," Dusty said, as he got ready to skin it. "I reckon yah know how much I dislike destroyin' any of your critters, but I promise, I'll use every usable part." With that said, Dusty got to work.

After skinning and quartering the moose, he then addressed the problem of getting it back to town. He knew that he wouldn't be able to take it all with him, so he decided to cache the bigger share of it high up in one of the nearby spruce trees. After fulfilling this task to his satisfaction, he and Shadow Spirit ate squaw candy[8] and hard tack, as they started back down the trail to Hope.

As darkness settled over the vast untamed wilderness, Dusty was disappointed at the amount of trail he struggled over in the short amount of daylight allotted him on this cold winter's day in Alaska. In the past four hours of gray, cold light, he was sure the distance wasn't more than a mile, and probably closer to a half mile.

The wind came up and at times blew ice crystals in Dusty's face like thousands of needles hitting his leathery skin. This in itself, Dusty had grown use to since he came

to the north country. What was really ticking him off was the fact he wasn't going to make it back to his cabin by supper time, and that meant he would have to eat his own fixin's one more night, ... Well, that's not really the whole truth either. Since the Christmas party at the general store a month or so ago, ole

Dusty had been doing a heap of sparking with Aura Lee. Every time his thoughts would turn to her, and that was more often than he would admit, his ole heart would go to beating like an Indian war drum and his mind turned to mush.

Just before Dusty left to hunt up fresh meat for the town, she had promised him she would come over and fix him a home cooked meal that would knock his hat in the creek.

As total darkness surrounded him and his great wolf-dog, Shadow Spirit, Dusty went about getting a fire going, and coffee boiling. "Well ole girl," he said to her as he worked, "if this here wind hadn't come up, we sure enough would've tried to make the cabin even in the dark." Shadow was laying by the now, warm fire, looking at Dusty with ears forward, as if she knew every word he was saying.

Over the past months, the bond between Dusty and Shadow Spirit had grown so strong, that when you saw one, the other was always close by. Most of the time if you asked Dusty about the obvious affection between them, he'd say. "Ah she's just an ole wolf-dog taken to followin' me aroun'." But everyone knew different. I'd sure pity the person who tried to lay a hand on that ole wolf-dog.

There was a gentleness about Dusty and he had an uncanny way with animals, but at the same time, you knew if he had to be, he could be as tough as a grizzly and twice as ornery. Dusty warmed himself with a strong steaming cup of coffee and noticed the stars were becoming visible and the wind was dying down to a gentle breeze.

"Well, Shadow ole girl, maybe we stopped too soon. The moon ought ta be up in a couple of hours and it's goin' ta be full. What say we pack up and hit the trail?" In one bounding leap, Shadow was right smack dab in the middle of him. All excited and raring to go.

"I take it by all this commotion, you're ready to hit the trail right now!" With that said, Dusty systematically started packing up, and in just a few minutes was ready to light shuck. The trail was barely visible as they started out. Dusty only had one thing … or should I say, one person on his mind. If he would have known what lay ahead of him this night, I'm sure he would have had second thoughts about starting out before the moon came up. Shadow was breaking trail as best she could, but the drifted snow in places became impossible to pass.

Finally Dusty called her back saying, "Maybe yah better let me do the trail breaking for a while, them ole drifts are givin' yah a heap of trouble." Dusty's admiration for his great white wolf-dog grew with each giant snow drift he had to fight his way through. When an open area appeared before him, Dusty was more than ready to take a breather. Ahead he saw a log jutting out of the snow and decided to set his tired bones on it to take a much needed rest. As he almost reached it, Shadow, a short ways behind him, started to bark and raise cane as if her tail was caught in a bear trap.

Dusty stopped in his tracks and spun around to see what the commotion was all about. ... In that instant he knew Shadow's warning had come too late. ...

❧ CHAPTER 5 ❧

Snow started falling shortly after Dusty and Shadow Spirit hit the trail. One Eyed Reilly had a bad feeling about it right from the start and decided to go talk to George Roll.

Trudging through the rapidly deepening snow, he reached the general store the same time as V.O. and several of the other concerned town folks. As usual, the store was cozy and warm, with the smell of fresh coffee. Unfortunately this spur-of-the-moment gathering wasn't one of a social nature. On the contrary, it was one of concern. No one had even called it, they just came to the store because they knew the others would be there. As in the past, whenever there was trouble, this was the place to come.

"This storm is turnin' into a mean one," George

was saying, as One Eye was shaking the snow off his parka. "Dusty could be in real trouble and we. …"

At that moment the door flung open and in rushed Aura Lee. "I told all of you something might happen, and now look. It's a blizzard out there and Dusty is caught in it!"

The room fell silent. No one looked her in the eye because of the guilt they were feeling. When One Eye started speaking, it surprised everyone in the room. Generally he was a man of few words and only spoke up when he had something important to say. "As I see it," he said "one of us needs to be a doin', instead of jawin'! … I knew all of yah would be down here, so I come down ta tell yah I'm a fixin' ta hitch up my dogs and go fetch him back here … Don't no one try to change my mind, cause I'm a goin'!"

Before anyone could react to One Eye's short, and to the point statement, he was out the door.

Back at his cabin, One Eye hurriedly threw together what he would need to survive while searching for Dusty, and then went outside to hitch up his dog team. With all but his eyes bundled up, he gave the command to mush and headed north along the trail toward Chickaloon Bay.

It was mid-morning when trouble struck. With One Eye's vision limited by his patch, he didn't see the tree across the trail until it was too late to stop his team from getting tangled in the branches. The abrupt stop threw him headlong into a snow drift. This would have been hilarious if he wasn't on such an urgent mission, but time was of the essence and this delay could be very costly.

His dogs were veterans and knew not to fight the entanglement. In a short time, One Eye had them untangled and the sled righted, but then the hard part started. The huge tree had the entire trail blocked and there was no visible way around. The only thing to do was get the old ax out and try to chop his way through it. After three hours of nonstop chopping, One Eye realized he needed help. The tree was just too big to cut through with an ax. When he came to this conclusion, he decided to start for town. The dogs had rested while he worked on the tree and were ready and willing to head back.

Knowing that darkness was fast approaching and danger lurked around every bend in the trail, One Eye kept a grueling pace. As darkness finally swathed the land, the wind had died to a gentle murmur and the snow fall was almost nonexistent. "Well if luck holds," One Eye said, to himself, "I reckon we should hit town 'afore the moon comes up."

Looking into the night sky, One Eye saw patches where the clouds were giving way to the twinkle of stars, shining like diamonds on a black velvet cloth. Less than an hour went by before One Eye topped the last ridge and saw the lights of town below. In a matter of minutes, he was bringing his team to a stop in front of the store.

Someone had seen him coming, and the people inside charged headlong through the door in excited anticipation, only to be disappointed when they discovered One Eye hadn't found Dusty. After telling of the fallen tree blocking the trail and how he tried to get through it with an ax, the tone in One Eye's voice changed. When he spoke next, it was with a gentle plea to his voice that no one had ever heard before. "I reckon all of yah know what I'm fixin' ta ask and I surely wouldn't be a askin' if I could've got through that there tree by myself ... but, but I need help. I need someone to help me cut a trail through that there tree."

The silence that fell in the room was electrified with tension or maybe should I say ... guilt? What ever it was, it was broken when V.O.'s voice brought everyone back to the task at hand. "You can count on me." He said. "It's time someone around here found some grit. Miss Aura Lee was right, we should have never let Dusty go, he could be seriously hurt, or God forbid ... dead. One Eye, I'll have my team hitched in twenty minutes. I'm sure Charley will let you use his dogs, yours have to be wore plum out. We can get a block and tackle at the Smithy's and I'll bring my whip saw ... why, we'll be through that tree like a hot knife through butter."

Turning to Aura Lee he said. "You just rest easy, we'll be back in no time with Dusty safe and sound." Even though One Eye was exhausted, he moved with utmost speed and was ready to leave with V.O.. The sleds were loaded with provisions and tools and the moon was on the rise as One Eye and V.O. headed north toward Chickaloon Bay.

In the distance they could hear the plaintive call of a lone wolf. ...

⇒ CHAPTER 6 ⇒

The ground violently pitched Dusty about like a rag doll, he grabbed for the log he had been standing close to, but it too was being tossed about. At that instant a cracking, grinding sound came to his ears and a cavernous crack opened at his feet. Looking down, Dusty saw cold murky water and realized the place he had chosen to rest wasn't a clearing at all. ... It was a small lake!

Looking about, after the ground stopped shaking, Dusty saw the awesome power and destruction of an earthquake and wondered if there was more to come. The crack in the ice was a formidable barrier, and as he assessed his situation, what he found made it worse—Much worse. To his dismay, he discovered the crack encircled him completely. As Dusty mulled this over, his small, unstable island shuttered violently, knocking him to his knees. He didn't have time to think, he only had time too react.

Springing to his feet in one smooth motion, he leaped for the other side of the cavernous crack that was even wider now. Dusty knew in that moment he had made a grievous mistake. ... He wasn't going to make it! Reaching with all his strength, he grabbed for the edge of the crevasse as he hurled by it, heading for the icy cold splash, and the inevitable freezing death, that awaited him in the murky water below.

To his surprise though, Dusty felt his hands hit the ice with a body jarring smack, and then the scramble was on. His purchase was minimal at best and he knew his life depended on his own strength to pull him over the edge of this ice crevasse.

Dusty wasn't a big man, he stood only five foot six inches, but was broad across the shoulders, had a barrel chest, and arms as strong as a grizzly bear. Hopefully this strength would be enough to save him from a freezing, watery grave. With all the might he could muster, he began to pull himself, inch by inch over the edge. Somewhere in the distances Dusty could hear the frantic barking of Shadow Spirit and for a moment wondered what she was barking at.

His struggle and the cold was taking it's toll. He could feel his arms weakening. Trying to get a better hold on the ice, he started to slip. Terror struck his heart and many things came flashing through his mind at that moment. He didn't see the powerful hand reach down and clutch his wrist with a vise like grip. The next thing he knew, he was being pulled to safety by a giant of a man.

The Indian looked down at Dusty with a hostile look, and in that brief moment, the thought crossed his mind that he was saved from a freezing death, only to die a tortured one at the hands of this menace standing over him.

In the next instant all fear left Dusty as a warm, gentle grin lit the huge Indian's face. His eyes showed concern when he asked in perfect English. "Are you hurt my friend? When the earth moved, as it often does here along the great water (Turnagain Arm), I feared you were lost and all that I had done for you, that my spirit had told me to do in the past, had been for nothing. If your faithful companion and my long time friend, the one I call Strong Heart and you call Shadow Spirit, hadn't led me to you, I am sure your life would have ended this day."

Dusty didn't know what to say. He was flabbergasted. How did this stranger know he called his wolf-dog Shadow Spirit? ... And what did he mean by, "all the things he's done for me in the past?"

"Say, how is it yah know Shadow Spirit's name?" Dusty started to question. "How is it that I ain't never seen yah around 'afore?... Who are yah anyway?"

The Indian held up a big hand, putting a stop to Dusty's questions. "I will tell you answers to your many questions, but we must leave here before the ground shakes again, and we are trapped here on the ice. My camp isn't far. You can warm yourself by my fire, and have some hot coffee. There I will give you answers to all your questions and more."

The hike to the Indian's camp was short. It amazed Dusty how short. He considered himself an alert woodsman and how he had missed the trail leading off the main one he had earlier traversed, was beyond his comprehension.

The camp, located in a clearing next to a small stream, was neat and inviting. Without the Indian, the fire had burned low. The coffee, sitting next to the coals, was still hot and Dusty gratefully accepted a full, steaming tin cup.

As he collected his thoughts and was forming

the questions which needed answers, the Indian began speaking. "Many winters ago I was banished from my village for being a friend to a Tlingit. They are our enemies from the south and to befriend one is unforgivable. He had been attacked by the great bear, just as you had been, and needed my help. I took him to the same cave I took you to and stayed with him for several suns—I mean days. He had been mauled badly and I could not help him. He died one morning while I was hunting food.

"While trying to save the Tlingit's life, an evil man from our village was spying on me. When I returned, I was taken before the tribal council and banished from my people."

As Dusty listened, many things became clear to him for the first time. "Since yah saved me from that grizz. …"

"No!" The Athabascan said. "I did not save you. … Great Heart, I mean Shadow Spirit did. She ran that bear off then kept watch over you. I only brought you to my cave and took care of you until you regained your strength."

"Why did yah not show yourself?" Dusty asked.

"I did not know if you were friend or enemy,

so I decided it would be best to stay out of sight and continue to help you from afar. After you recovered, there was no need for me to reveal myself, but my heart was worried that I may have helped an evil man, that I should have let die. ... I have been watching you ever since.

"When you volunteered, at your town meeting, to hunt food for your village, I was outside the window. I knew then I had done the right thing— You have a good heart Dusty Sourdough!"

Dusty and his new friend talked a while longer. Shadow Spirit made herself comfortable by the fire, and in no time she was sound asleep, as if nothing out of the ordinary had happened. Dusty too became sleepy and dozed by the warm fire. Something hitting the ground next to him startled him awake.

"Easy," came the voice of the Indian. "It is only I. ... While you dozed, I returned to the frozen lake and retrieved your gear. When light comes in the morning, you will have everything you need to continue your journey."

Dusty woke to the sound of familiar voices coming from down the trail. He couldn't believe his eyes when the sleds came into sight, carrying his two friends.

"Well I'll be!" Dusty exclaimed. "If yah two ain't a sight fer sore eyes. Boy! when that shaker hit yesterday, I thought I was a goner. If it weren't fer my Indian friend here. ..." Dusty stopped in mid-sentence. Looking about, he discovered the Indian was gone.

"What Indian?" V.O. questioned. "There isn't anyone here but us. Maybe you dreamed it! ... Sometimes your mind can play tricks on yah out here."

"No!... I didn't imagine this, he was here, he saved my life!"

"What's this feller look like?" One Eye asked. As Dusty described the Indian, his friends got puzzled looks. The description matched no one they knew or had ever seen.

"Does this friend of yours have a name?" Asked V.O. This question stopped Dusty cold. In their conversation around the fire, the night before, he had neglected to ask that very question.

"I... I don't know his name, he never told me... but he was here, I know I wasn't imagining him—he was here!"

"Well, whether or not he's real, we can talk about it back in the warmth of George's store.

Right now I think we should hit the trail." One Eye said, with finality in his voice.

Before they started back, Dusty told of his successful hunt. After returning to his cache and loading the moose meat on the two sleds, they headed down their back trail toward home.

The return trip was uneventful. With the dog teams pulling the load, it was much faster than the trip out. The conversation was minimal, and the subject of the Indian never came up. As they topped the final ridge, and town was in sight, something made Dusty turn and look back. To his surprise, standing at the edge of the forest was his Indian friend. There wasn't any doubt in his mind now that he was real and Dusty knew they would meet again. ...

⇌ CHAPTER 7 ⇌

It was like a fourth of July celebration in the spring. Everyone in town was in a festive mood.

Just knowing Dusty was back and unhurt was enough to lift the town's spirit, but when they found out the hunt was successful, the people exploded with joy.

Everyone decided the occasion called for a get-together, a potluck and dance at the general store, but unlike the last one. Dusty didn't need his arm twisted this time to attend. He was all for it. The shindig was set for the following night and Dusty knew Aura Lee would be there. Anyway he hoped she would be.

Upon his return the whole town had gathered about him—everyone that is, except Aura Lee.

When he looked about, he caught a glimpse of her through the crowd. She had tears in her eyes, and when she saw him looking at her, she turned and ran away.

Dusty didn't understand her actions. They certainly put a damper on his enthusiasm. For some reason, he didn't quite comprehend. She was the only one he really wanted to see. After the task of dividing the meat among the town, Dusty headed for One Eye's cabin, and a well-deserved night of rest.

The sun was high in the cloudless, Alaska blue sky, when Dusty woke from his restful sleep. "Well, it's about time yah rolled out!" One Eyed Reilly said with a humorous chuckle. "I got the makin's all mixed up fer some of them there sourdough flapjacks yah favor. I reckon I ought ta call them; Dusty's Sourdough Flapjacks. Shucks, if everybody outside[9] would take a likin' to um like you, I wouldn't hav' ta work my fingers ta the bone a lookin' for gold anymore.

"Durned if yah don't come up with some rip snorten ides!" Dusty good-naturedly retorted. "One of these days, I do believe, you're gonna come up with a newfangled idee that'll put some gold in yur poke." They both had a good laugh over this thought. Shadow Spirit even got into the act with a few joyous barks.

The day went by quickly and before they knew it, the sky to the west was aglow with the setting sun. ... Such beauty, Dusty thought, as he watched the sky change from a golden orange to a fiery red. "All this and still my heart has an empty place in it," he said, to his ever faithful companion, Shadow Spirit. "Well girl, maybe I'll figure it out someday. I fer sure need somethin' in my life. I just can't imagine what it could be."

Almost everyone in town was at the store when Dusty and One Eye walked in. The smells were tantalizing and the jubilation in the air was overpowering. The children played hide and seek behind the drygoods, while the ladies finished laying out their finest recipes. The men gathered around the old potbellied stove, listening to V.O. Rollie tell how he and One Eye found Dusty.

As soon as they spotted him, cheers went up, and Dusty became the center of attention. Dusty didn't really like all the fuss being raised about him. By nature he was shy and kept to himself. He felt as if everyone was staring at him and he didn't know what to say.

"Good-evening!" A voice came from behind him.

Recognizing the voice, Dusty spun around with a smile on his face, as well as one of relief, to see Aura Lee coming toward him. She was absolutely the most beautiful lady he had ever seen. Her smile lit up the whole room, and gave Dusty a warm feeling all over.

"Good-evenin' Ma'am!. … You're bout as perty as the sun risin' on a spring mornin'!" Dusty said, turning red with embarrassment. "I was affeered yah weren't gonna come ta night."

"Well … well I got something in my eye and had to go home … I'm sorry if you thought I was mad about something." Aura Lee hoped her explanation would be adequate and Dusty wouldn't ask her to explain.

When Aura Lee finished speaking, Dusty saw something in her eyes. Perhaps a plea, he wasn't sure. What ever it was, he chalked it up to his not being able to figure out women. When everyone had their fill of all the wonderful food, a fiddle and mouth harp appeared, and music began. Throughout the evening, Dusty and Aura Lee were inseparable. It left no doubt in anyone's mind that love was in bloom.

If Dusty wasn't careful he would be the first guy to get hitched in a place called Hope. … …

⤜ CHAPTER 8 ⤛

As spring came to Hope, love came to Dusty and Aura Lee. They spent their spare time together. When school let out in the afternoons, they would wander off with Shadow Spirit by their side and a picnic basket swinging from Dusty's arm. The days were growing longer and Dusty felt a peace that had never been there before. His life was tranquil, but the beauty of Alaska in the spring, visible in every direction, was about to change.

It was one such afternoon that brought Dusty and Aura Lee on the threshold of death. ...

As Dusty came down the trail leading to the school, the bell hanging outside began ringing with all the gusto a young feller could muster, knowing it meant school was out for another day.

"Good afternoon young feller!" Dusty said with a smile. "It looks ta me like your mighty happy school is out fer another day! Why shucks! Back when I wasn't any bigger un you, my grandpa would hav ta warm the seat of my britches pert near every week, cause I'd play hooky and go fishin' instead of a doin my book learnin' … I surely do wish I'd a listened to him. A feller needs ta do figurin' and know how ta read and write in this here world."

Dusty looked down at the lad and smiled. He had a special place in his heart for little ones and somehow they knew it. At times, all the kids in town gathered around him, listening in awe, while he told stories of the Wild West. Dusty had taken a special likin' to this little guy, who by coincidence, was without a father. Dusty didn't know the whole story, but he did know he had left to go huntin' and never came back.

The wilderness is beautiful but unforgiving. A wrong decision or a misplaced step could mean disaster. In this case it left this freckle-faced boy without a father and, his mother without a husband.

"You'd better get on home and get your chores done. There ought ta be a heap a light left ta go fishin' when yah get done."

"Yes sir!" the young feller said, and was off like a shot down the trail.

Shadow Spirit loved to play with the kids and the feeling was mutual. She spent hours romping through the spring grass with them, so when the kids came out Dusty paid little attention as she went running off to play. Dusty knew she would catch up if she wanted to come along.

Dusty turned in time to see Aura Lee, a smile on her face and a bounce to her step, come out of the school. As usual, just like the first time he laid eyes on her, his heart started beating like an Indian war drum. "Howdy! I just came by ta see if you'd like to go have a look at a little somethin' I been a doin'? It's not too fer from here and yah might be a likin' it!"

"I have test papers to grade, Dusty, but if it won't take long. ..."

That's all Dusty needed to hear. Taking her by the hand, he headed down a trail toward a meadow where they had picnicked once. Aura Lee really loved this place, with a crystal clear stream running through it, and tall fir trees all about.

When they were close to the meadow, Dusty

stopped and blindfolded Aura Lee. Telling her that what he had to show her was a surprise, and boy was it! In a matter of minutes, Dusty and Aura Lee stepped into a clearing. Dusty, removing the covering from her eyes said. "Well what da yah think?"

Aura Lee stood there speechless, not believing her eyes. Before her stood a beautiful cabin in the finishing stages. The first thing she noticed was the covered porch stretching the entire front of the cabin. From the porch was the view of a small meadow with a small creek gurgling by, about two hundred yards away. "Do yah like it?. ... Come on inside ... I, ... I built as best as I could remember." Dusty stammered.

"Remember what?" Aura Lee asked, and then it hit her like a sack of grain.

From the moment the blindfold was removed something looked familiar about this cabin. ... It was like the one she had always dreamed of, like the one she had told Dusty she would like someday. "Oh it's beautiful Dusty! It's just like the one I have dreamed of so many times!"

In the main room was a big spacious kitchen with a brand new wood cook-stove up against the right side. Next to it, was a long pine counter, with shelves above and below. The front wall had a large window that enjoyed the same view as the porch. Under the window was another counter and further down the wall was a huge pantry, with four cedar doors. Dusty had built a plank table, sitting close to the window. The main room was spacious and airy too.

The ceiling was open-beamed with hand carved fitted logs. At the far end was a beautiful fireplace made of river rock. Dusty had taken weeks to select and carry up for the building of it. Halfway down the left wall, a stairway led to the second floor and what was to be the two bedrooms. The larger one had a wardrobe closet and a partially built frame of a bed in it. The other room was much smaller and bare of any furnishing.

The smell of the fresh cut logs and the afternoon sun streaming through the open windows made it all the more beautiful. To Dusty the finishing touch was standing next to him looking around at his labor of love, for he had built this for her, and her alone.

"I sure do hope yah like it, causin' I have somethin' else I been a meanin' ta ask yah ... I mean I've been a wonderin'. ... I mean do yah think ... Aha shucks! A perty lady like you would never think of a marryin' an ole crusty good fer nothin' like me. I ain't. ... ..."

Dusty didn't have time to finish, Aura Lee threw her arms around his neck saying. "Yes, yes Dusty. Yes! Oh Dusty, you're not a crusty good for nothing. I've loved you since your first, 'howdy ma'am!' I was beginning to think you would never ask me. ... Come on, let's get back to town so I can tell everyone and start making plans for our wedding!.. Dusty you have made me the happiest girl in the whole world."

Dusty too, was happy beyond belief. Stepping over the threshold, with Aura Lee in hand, Dusty failed to notice a subtle change in the surrounding forest. Any other time he would have picked up on it immediately. The sounds of the forest were nonexistent. It was as if all the birds and critters were hiding in fear for their lives. If Dusty would have noticed this, maybe the next thing that happened, could have been avoided.

A blood curdling roar came from along side of the cabin! In one easy motion Dusty turned to face his tormentor and at the same time, grabbed Aura Lee and shoved her toward the door of the cabin. Then it charged! ... Pulling his Colt he fired at almost point blank range at the biggest, meanest grizzly he had ever had the misfortune of meeting up with. The shot hit the bear dead center, but it kept coming. The shot hadn't slowed him one step.

Dusty stepped backward just as the bear took a swipe at him with his lethal front paw. The razor sharp claws caught Dusty a glancing blow to his shoulder and knocked him to the ground. With cat like speed, Dusty rolled to the side and sprang to his feet. This seemed to confuse the griz for a moment and that moment was all Dusty needed to get his knife out.

The grizzly let out another death defying roar and charged. This time Dusty didn't back up. Instead he lunged straight for the bear. Ducking a massive paw aimed for his head, he was in the grasp of this huge carnivore and could feel and smell his hot breath on the back of his neck. Dusty pulled in as close as he could to avoid the gaping jaws of the man killer. At the same time plunged his knife into the bear's rib cage.

The animal let out an ear shattering roar, but this time it was different, this time it was one of pain. Still the bear's grip was literally hugging the life out of Dusty and he became light headed from lack of air. He knew time was running out. He had to hit a vital spot with his knife if he had any hopes to survive.

The bear again was trying to get at Dusty with his powerful jaws. Looking up he could only see fur and more fur. This was it, and Dusty knew it.

When the bear's ugly yellow teeth were just inches from his face, Dusty stabbed his knife upward into the mass of fur where he thought the bear's throat might be. To his surprise the bear gave out a roar and released his death hold on Dusty! As he slipped free, the griz started falling forward and Dusty knew he could never get out of the way. He had lost too much blood and his strength was slipping away.

The last thing he remembered, before the smothering weight of the bear crushed the consciousness from him, was a familiar voice he recognized—and it wasn't Aura Lee's. ...

⨯ CHAPTER 9 ⨯

Slowly Dusty became aware of voices and then light. Opening his eyes he found himself looking into the face of his mysterious Indian friend.

"Lay still my friend, while I finish bandaging these wounds," said the Indian. "That old rogue griz didn't do as much damage as the last time, but that doesn't mean he didn't get in a few good licks. ... Lucky you were out cold, that way it was easy for Miss Aura Lee to hold you down while I used a porcupine quill and sinew to sew up your shoulder. That ole griz laid it open clean to the bone!"

"I guess it could-a been worse," Dusty said. "He coulda taken my head off!"

"I reckon he was still mad at you for waking

him up early last winter before he got all his beauty sleep."[10]

"How do yah figure he's the same one that was in the cave?" Dusty asked his Indian friend.

"Two reasons," he said. "One, that griz in the cave had only three toes on his right, front paw, like the one you just killed. The second reason, is this piece of arrow I dug out of his neck. I put it there myself when he was on the run from that cave!"

"He was one mean bear, and I doubt you were his first human victim, you were just the one that got away. Speaking of getting away! I never in my born day seen anything like it, the way you wrestled that griz I mean! In my village you'd be honored as one with great powers. When what you have done becomes known, there will be no one that doesn't know the name of Dusty Sourdough ... The one who slays grizzlies with his bare hands!"

"Speakin' of names? ... What handle do yah go by? ... It seems ta me, I oughter know the feller's name who's pulled my bacon out of the fire three different times!"

"My Indian name, in your language means, One

Who Walks Alone. I was givin' that name when I was banished from my village."

"I reckon it's 'bout time you get a new one then, cause as long as ole Dusty is a kickin', you won't be a needin' a handle like that. No friend of mine ever has ta walk alone!. ... I'll just shorten it some ... How 'bout Walker? If'n yar needin' it longer ... How's Walker?... Dusty's friend!"

Aura Lee had been listening to the conversation and it never ceased to amaze her how gentle a spirit Dusty had and yet how tough he could be when the occasion called for it. "After ... Walker ... and I skin and butcher that brute," Aura Lee said "do you think you have the strength to make it back to town?"

"Why sure!" Dusty said, with a little indignation in his voice. "I'll even skin that ornery critter myself. ... I feel fine! I've gotten hurt worse tryin' ta shave, ... That's why I got this beard!"

Aura Lee and Walker saw it would be useless to try to persuade Dusty to rest, even though they knew he was in a great deal of pain.

Even though skinning and dressing a griz is a tall order, it didn't take as long as it would have, with only one person doing it. Aura Lee surprised Dusty when she rolled up her sleeves and began skinning as fast as any seasoned skinner. By dark they had the job done, and stored the meat in a cache Dusty built behind the cabin. The meat would have to be salted, smoked, and preserved as soon as possible, but for now, this would have to do.

~~~

After the town folks met Dusty's mysterious Indian friend and heard about the bear attack, they stood in amazement that Dusty had escaped with his life. Except for the claw marks on his shoulder, he appeared to be unhurt.

After a few more questions Dusty stood up and said with a tiredness to his voice. "I'm a gonna get me a little shut-eye. Walker, you're more than welcome ta stay with One Eye and me … Good-night Miss Aura Lee, see yah in the morn!"

With that said, Dusty turned and headed for the door, but as he opened it and started to step through, he turned around to say one last thing. "Me un Miss Aura Lee are a fixin' ta get hitched." Not another word was spoken, he stepped out the door and gently closed it behind himself.

No one heard him softly humming the song;

Aura Lee,[11] or saw the smile of contentment on his face as he looked into the star filled heavens of an Alaska night. ...

The Reverend Hill would be making his circuit through Hope the last Sunday of the month, so Dusty and Aura Lee decided to marry on that day, April 30, 1888. This would be the first wedding ever to be held in Hope and the people were going to do it right.

The church was decorated by the ladies, using lace and brightly colored ribbons in place of flowers. Even though it was the beginning of spring, it was still too early for wild flowers, or even fireweed to be blooming.

Everyone in town planned on being at the wedding. Even Johnny Dynamite O'Brien was due up the Cannon Ball[12] with supplies for the town. He, being one of Dusty's friends, would want to attend the wedding. Dusty planned on booking passage for himself and Aura Lee on the Utopia to take her to Wrangell and Skagway for their honeymoon. This was the last stop for Johnny before his return voyage to Seattle, so there should be plenty of room on board.

The days before the wedding went by quickly. When the Reverend was spotted on the trail leading to town, it took everyone by surprise. In the past, he usually came by way of boat, with Johnny Dynamite, on the Utopia.

Over a cup of coffee at George Roll's general store, the Reverend explained, "Coming up from Skagway we had to stop at Homer, on Kachemak Bay. The ice in Cook Inlet prevented us from proceeding up the Arm. While waiting there, Captain O'Brien took gravely ill!

"Among the passengers on board was a miner who had once followed a medical practice. He said the Captain had acute appendicitis and needed it removed. Then he told us he hadn't performed an operation in over five years and wasn't sure he could do it. Being the only one around with any doctoring ability, the Captain offered him $1,000.00 as a fee, and he agreed to try.

"The only place clean enough to operate was Mrs. Bank's gallery home on the Spit, so without delay we moved him to it. After liberally applying him with the only anesthetic around—whiskey, the doctor began the operation. The only tools available to perform this, were a pair of scissors, a kitchen knife, a forecastle needle and thread, and a bucket of hot water. "When the operation was over, the doc didn't give the Captain much of a chance. "I can't do no more for him. Keep him clean and make him rest." He said. "I'm strikin' out for the gold fields."

The Reverend took a long drink of his coffee and then continued. "One of the other passengers on the Utopia, a well-mannered, pleasant, dark haired man going by the name of Smith, said he would watch over him and serve as his nurse until the Captain recovered or went under.

"Even though Mr. Smith seemed like a gentle, peace loving guy," he continued "I sure wouldn't want to upset him. He carried two pearl handled revolvers under his frock coat and I got a feeling he knows how to use um! To get here in time for your wedding Dusty; I left on foot, the next morning."

Dusty was concerned about Captain O'Brien. His boat, the Utopia, was the one he had boarded in Seattle to come north to Alaska. On the voyage, he and the fiery, little Irish sea captain, had become friends. They had passed long nights in the wheelhouse, talking of days gone by. As soon as he and Aura

Lee were hitched, he decided they would light shuck and head overland to Homer. His friend might need his help, and besides—it was on the trail To Wrangell!

≈ CHAPTER 10 ≈

If the weather was any indication of how the wedding was going to go, it would be magnificent! The Arm was calm and shimmered like a mirror of gold in the early morning sun. It reflected the majestic, snowcapped mountains, and in the azure blue sky, a great bald eagle drifted on the currents. It was a one-of-a-kind painting by the master, that could only be found in Alaska.

The little log church was filled to overflowing. Reverend Hill was well liked and always gave uplifting sermons. Hope is a God fearing community, so it wasn't unusual to have the church filled to capacity.

This Sunday though was different, the ladies were in their Sunday best, but with a few added touches. Glittering brooches or other fine jewelry, for only the most special occasions appeared. Even the little girls had colorful ribbons and lace adornments in their hair.

Immediately following the services, the atmosphere changed to one of festivity and anticipation of the wedding to come. No one had seen Dusty or Aura Lee since late Friday when the Reverend had come to town. Everyone was curious, wondering what they would look like in their wedding garb.

The Reverend called the congregation to order. The church door opened and in walked Dusty and his best man, One Eyed Reilly. You could have heard a pin drop. The look on everyone's face was worth a thousand words. The two men walking up the aisle looked nothing like the One Eyed Reilly or Dusty Sourdough they knew. Dusty had traded his familiar buckskins for a gray frock coat, black tie, and tucked into the top of highly polished cavalry boots, a pair of freshly brushed black trousers. Both men had neatly trimmed beards—and it was obvious they had both taken a trip to the creek!

When the two reached the front of the church, the Reverend stepped forward and Mrs. Roll began to play the wedding march on the old church pump organ. Everyone stood and looked to the rear of the church as Aura Lee, on the arm of V.O. Rollie, whom she had asked to give her away, started up the aisle.

The Indian war drums started beating in Dusty's chest the minute his eyes fell on her. She was beautiful! Her gown was pure white satin and trimmed with delicate lace. She had an ivory cameo on a red velvet ribbon about her neck, and the bridal bouquet she carried, was made of silk red roses.

The ceremony went smoothly until the Reverend got to the part ..."Dusty Sou..., Dusty?" he asked, "What's your real last name? It can't be Sourdough!"

"Well preacher..." Dusty said hesitantly. "I reckon if yah need ta know it ta get us hitched, I'll hav ta tell yah. I already told Aura Lee, I ain't in trouble with the law or anything like that. It's just that it's the same name as a famous feller down Texas way, and people kept mistakin' me fer him ... so I changed it! I'd be right grateful if ya'd keep it ta yourself.

Reverend Hill gave his word that he would, so Dusty bent forward and whispered it in his ear. The preacher took an involuntary step backwards. He had a look of surprise on his face, and as he spoke, his voice cracked. After clearing his throat, he finished the ceremony and it seemed as if everyone had forgotten the incident by the time the reception got underway.

The reception went on all day, and as usual the food was beyond description. Mrs. Roll baked a beautiful wedding cake and V.O. prepared an open pit barbecue of moose and other wild game. There were fresh baked cookies and birch candy for the kids, along with chocolate flavored milk to drink. When people weren't eating, they were participating in the competitive games, such as sack races for the energetic, and horseshoes for the ones who ate too much.

The whole day was filled with joy. One of the most moving moments was when Aura Lee's entire class presented her with the most precious wedding gift of all. The class knew ... or should I say, felt the love Aura Lee had for children. They knew Dusty shared this same love because he was always telling stories of the Old West to the girls and boys that gathered around and sat at his feet to hear his tales of daring.

The children waited till last, it took two of the older boys to carry it in. When Aura Lee carefully removed the wrappings from the gift, tears wailed up in her eyes. Dusty put his arms around her and his eyes too, were puddling up. There before them, was the most beautiful cradle any mother could hope for. The boys, instead of going fishing after school, had taken turns working on the cradle. At the same time, the girls had sewn the most precious baby-quilt you ever laid your eyes on. One of the girls spoke for the whole class, "We all hope you and Dusty have at least a dozen young uns', Miss Aura Lee." This made Aura Lee and Dusty blush red with embarrassment.

As the day drew to a close and another page in the life of Dusty Sourdough's trail to destiny was completed, Dusty knew wherever that trail led next, it would be shared with the love of his life—for better or worse—his destiny would become part of her's.

The sun was setting as Dusty carried Aura Lee over the threshold of their new cabin. In the few weeks before their wedding, Dusty had time to finish up the remaining work on it. Thanks to their friends, it was furnished with all the things they needed to make life comfortable. Someone had slipped away from the festivities early and had a cheerful fire going in the big river rock fireplace, making the cabin warm and inviting to the newlyweds.

Morning comes early for Alaskans and it found

Dusty and his new bride in the kitchen preparing their first breakfast together. Aura Lee had the bacon sliced and sizzling in a big iron skillet, while Dusty ground up his special blend of coffee beans.

Shadow Spirit didn't quite know what to make of the new arrangement, all she understood was that the two people she loved most in the world, were here, together! The smells of breakfast cooking made her lick her chops and with any luck she figured, if she put on her best lovable puppy look, maybe ... just maybe, Aura Lee would give her a handout.

"Look at that rascal!" Dusty said with a chuckle. "Ya'd think she was spoiled!"

"Dusty you may fool everybody else, but I've seen you with that wolf-dog and I know, without a doubt, she has you wrapped around her paw. I'm surprised you don't have a place set for her at the table!" Aura Lee tried to keep a straight face when she finished saying this, but when she saw the look of innocence on Dusty's face, she broke into uncontrollable laughter.

During breakfast Dusty and Aura Lee discussed going overland to Homer. Dusty hoped Captain O'Brien had survived his operation and was on the mend. The sooner they left, the sooner he

could put his mind at ease. Aura Lee sensed the
urgency of Dusty's feelings, so she agreed they
should leave in the morning, at first light. ...
After all, this trip was her honeymoon too!

The rest of the day was spent getting ready for
their journey. If everything went well, it should
take them eight to ten days to reach Homer. As
Dusty packed grub and other essentials they
would need on the trail, he started feeling the
weight of responsibility.

"Well ole girl!" He exclaimed to Shadow Spirit. "We
gotta take real special care of our lady on this here
adventure." Dusty reached down and gave the
great white wolf-dog a loving pat. "Yah help ole
Dusty keep her safe... Okay?"

Shadow Spirit, as if understanding Dusty's words,
gave a sharp bark and ran into the bedroom
where Aura Lee was packing a few things in her
backpack. By the time they were packed and
ready to leave in the morning, the sun was
casting the long shadows of evening through
the forest and the sky to the west was turning
a brilliant red-orange.

Dusty was outside chopping wood and Aura
Lee was bustling about in her new kitchen. She
was preparing a supper of moose steaks, green
beans, she had bottled up the summer before,

boiled potatoes, and for dessert, her specialty, dried apple pie.

When Dusty finished splitting and stacking the wood, he rested on the porch enjoying the panoramic view and the wonderful smells coming from the kitchen.

Whap! ... "Dog-gone mosquitoes!" Dusty exclaimed. "Those little blood suckers are sure enough hungry! ... Whap! ... I reckon we'd better go in before these flyin' critters decide ta pack us off," he said to Shadow Spirit, who seemed unaffected by the winged pests.

Dusty couldn't remember ever enjoying a better meal, and when he told Aura Lee, she blushed with embarrassment and changed the subject. "I sure hope Mrs. Roll doesn't mind taking over my class while we're gone, those kids can be a hand full at times."

Yah don't have no need ta fret darlin'. Mrs. Roll wouldn't have offered if she didn't want to do it, and as far as handlin' them young uns' ... well, she handles George doesn't she?"

They both had a good laugh and that put Aura Lee's mind to rest. As the flames turned to red glowing embers in the fireplace, a warm, contented sleep came to Aura Lee and Dusty, cuddled in each others arms under their warm feather-tic quilt.

⇒ CHAPTER II ⇐

Dusty and Aura Lee woke to a misty, overcast morning. After a hardy breakfast and plenty of hot coffee, the couple hit the trail. Shadow Spirit ran ahead, chasing ground squirrels and frolicking through the forest on both sides of the trail. She loved running free and having the two humans along who encompassed her life, filled her heart with joy.

The first part of the trail, over Resurrection Pass, was easy going and pleasant. Trees and plants, dormant during the long cold winter were coming to life with new growth. The abundance of nature was visible everywhere. Before noon the clouds moved out and the sun shown in all it's glory.

Stopping beside an ice cold, fast moving stream for lunch, Dusty automatically looked for any fresh tracks. The usual ones were there: moose, wolf, Dall sheep, and then he spotted it … about twenty feet up stream Dusty found the foot print of a grizzly imprinted perfectly in the soft mud of the stream bank. This find in itself didn't bother him, but what bothered him, was the freshness of it.

As Dusty stood there looking at the huge paw print fill with water, he knew it was fresh—very fresh! Carefully looking about in all directions, and at the same time calling Shadow Spirit to his side, he tried to make a determination on this bear's intentions.

As Shadow Spirit approached Dusty, her hackles went up and she emitted a low growl from deep within. The scent of the grizzly was strong and it warned her the bear was close—too close for her liking.

"Easy girl," Dusty said softly, trying to soothe the big wolf-dog. "Maybe that ole bar will pay us no never mind and leave us alone. There ain't much we can do except keep a keen eye and hope that griz don't have a taste for people … or wolf-dog. We won't eat lunch here, if that critter gets a snout full of our victuals, we could be in a heap of trouble. Come on, let's light shuck and get away from here!"
Returning where he had left Aura Lee, he told

of his find. She needed to know of the danger and be prepared for what might happen. Dusty could see determination, along with fear, come into her eyes.

"Do you think it will try to follow us?" she asked.

"I reckon not, anyway I'm a hopin' not. That griz hasn't been out of hibernation too long, and more'n likely he's a headin' to lower territories where spring temperatures are warmer and food more plentiful. There are ornery ones though, like that ole rogue that liked the taste of my hide, but I've found if'n yah give 'um plenty a room they'll leave yah alone, and that's what we're a fixin' ta do! … We'll just hav' ta be careful."

Before starting up the trail, Dusty listened closely to the sounds of the surrounding forest. He could hear the symphony of spring all about, which was a good sign, for if a griz was lurking in the dense forest, all the critters and birds would be silent, fearing for their lives.

The sun had made most of it's journey across the brilliant blue sky when Dusty found a small spring to set up camp for the night. The site had a tranquil feel to it and firewood was plentiful, not only was there enough to build a cook fire with, there would be enough to keep a cozy warm fire going throughout the night.

How different it was to have Aura Lee along. For a moment he stood watching her scurry about collecting rocks for a fire-ring. Then she placed a flat one inside the ring. This was for the coffee pot to sit on and keep warm. Dusty was surprised, as well as impressed with Aura Lee's savvy of the wilderness. When Dusty had first laid eyes on her, he thought she was too delicate to know about living in the bush, let alone willing. Boy, was he wrong. She had taken to the trail as a duck takes to water. Aura Lee had a tasty supper ready in no time.

While eating and enjoying each other's company, Dusty kept a watchful eye on their back trail. He was a little worried the smells of Aura Lee's cooking would attract the griz, whose trail they had crossed earlier. When Dusty couldn't eat another bite, Aura Lee started cleaning up and securing the food in a bag, so Dusty could cache it high up, in a nearby tree.

While she did these things, Dusty scouted the perimeter of their camp before settling in for the night. He knew being familiar with the immediate surroundings could mean the difference between life and death. Even though it was spring, temperatures still dropped below freezing at night in the high country. As darkness caught up to the honeymooners, they snuggled close to each other by the cheery fire.

In the far off distance a mournful wolf howled and received an immediate answer by a plaintive howl of equal loneliness.

"Gee Dusty," Aura Lee said sweetly. "That wolf sounds so lonely. Do you think he was calling his mate and she was answering him?"

"Sure sweetheart, why ... wolves run in packs, like one big family. When yah hear em a howlin', that's just their way of talkin'! Take a look at Shadow Spirit. ... She knows what they're a talking about. I bet she could join right in, if she wanted to."

When Dusty mentioned Shadow Spirit's name, she lifted her head and looked at him with knowing eyes. Dusty knew without a doubt, Shadow Spirit did understand everything he said. He also knew the howling call of the wolves put a longing in the wolf part of her. A longing to return to the wild ... Maybe someday she would.

～～

The night passed without incident and the morning dawned to a cloudless sky. When Aura Lee opened her eyes, Dusty already had bacon frying on the fire, and a cup of coffee in his hand. "Good mornin' darlin'!" Dusty said. "I figured yah were plum tuckered out, so I let yah sleep in. Me and Shadow Spirit done took us a look about ta see if'n that griz might be a nosein' around. We went back down the trail a good five mile and didn't see hide nor hair of that critter. I reckon he decided we weren't worth the trouble."

Dusty and Aura Lee packed their gear after breakfast, returned their camp site to its pristine appearance, and then resumed their trek over Resurrection Pass.

By mid-morning the couple was above tree-line and the trail had become narrow and steep. Dusty remembered the trail led through a high mountain valley, and with a little luck they could make it by sundown. Dusty again was amazed at Aura Lee's grit, she was as rugged as she was pretty. He never had to wait on her, and not a complaint one ever crossed her lips.

When Dusty found a small spring trickling between the rocks, he called a halt for lunch. They had a fast meal of jerky, Johnny cakes, and cold spring water. It wasn't too tasty, but it filled the void and it was fast. The trail became even more treacherous as they made their way to the top of the pass. At times it was nothing more than a ledge on the face of a cliff. It was at these times when a misplaced step could mean a thousand foot fall to death.

The going slowed to a crawl in one of these spots, when an ear splitting scream came from Aura Lee. Dusty reached out for her and missed. In less than a heartbeat she was gone! He scrambled to the edge and was almost afraid to look over. The weak and shaken voice of Aura Lee came floating up to him. His heart leaped with joy! Looking over the edge he could see his love laying on a ledge about thirty feet below.

Shouting down he asked her, "Are yah all right? Can yah hear me? Oh please be all right!"

Aura Lee turned her face upward and giving Dusty a reassuring smile that didn't quite match her voice when she answered. "I … I think so, but I'm… I'm scared to move. Can you … I mean, how are you going to get me off this ledge?"

As Dusty listened, he could hear the fear in her voice, he too felt the same fear, but to dwell on it now could mean disaster. He swallowed hard and with a voice of confidence he answered. "I'll get yah up here, don't trouble your pretty little head about that. Yah just stay put and ole Dusty will have yah out of this here fix in a shake of a hound dog's tail!"

With that, Dusty stood and carefully removed his pack. Looking about he spotted what he needed. Just above the trail and to the left, was an outcrop of rocks. Taking his lasso off his pack, he looped it around what he hoped was the most secure rock of the bunch. Then he tugged on it with all his weight, and thankfully it held—so far.

After telling Aura Lee to protect her face, he dropped the lasso over the side. He told her to tie it around her waist and he would pull her up. The next thing that happened changed his plans completely.

With a shaky voice she told Dusty she didn't know how to tie a knot that would hold.

The only thing Dusty could figure out to do, was go down and get her. How he was going to do this ... well he wasn't sure. He had no choice. ... He had to do it! He took the rope in hand and eased himself over the edge. As he reached the precarious perch Aura Lee was clinging to, the solution to his problem came to him.

Holding the rope with one hand and reaching for Aura Lee with the other, he told her to get on his back and hang on tight. He wasn't sure he had the strength it would take to climb the rope with her on his back, but he could think of no other way. By the time he was halfway up, his arms and shoulders were burning from the strain. Looking up to see how much further he had to go, dirt and rocks came raining down in his face.

"Hey!" Dusty shouted, "Shadow Spirit, settle down up there! You're kickin' rocks down on us!" All of a sudden they were violently jerked about and it took all of Dusty's willpower to hang on. Next came a blood curdling roar … in that instant Dusty knew they were trapped. He couldn't hang there indefinitely and he didn't have the strength to go back down with Aura Lee on his back.

The giant grizz roared again and took another swipe at the rope. If he caught it clean with one of his claws they were goners. His claws were as sharp as a straight razor, and could cut through a rope like a hot knife through butter.

Shadow Spirit was a short distance ahead when she heard the grizzly's first roar. Then the faint sound of Dusty's voice came to her ears. She sprang into action, sprinting full tilt back down the trail. The grizzly was caught completely by surprise, and her tenacity threw him off balance. The grizzly had no equal in the forest and to have this wolf-dog attacking instead of running in fear was confusing him.

Again Shadow Spirit lunged at the bear and he

backed up. The fur was flying, claws flashing in the sun light, teeth snapping together. They found nothing but air!

The intense battle raged on, all the while Dusty and Aura Lee clung to life just a few feet below them. The bear caught Shadow Spirit a glancing blow that knocked the wind out of her. Not knowing he had only knocked the wind out of her, he moved in for the kill. Reaching down for her neck with gaping jaws he couldn't pull back fast enough to avoid the lighting speed of Shadow Spirit's razor sharp fangs, embedding into the bear's nose.

The startled grizzly roared in pain and bolted backward, tossing his head trying to dislodge the pain attached to the end of his nose. Disorientated with pain and not being able to shake Shadow Spirit's grip, the bear continued to try to back away from the excruciating pain, tossing his head back and fourth, and side to side. The final attempt came with one last violent shake of his massive head. He felt the hold loosen and took another step backward ... not knowing it would be his last!

Dusty took a chance and looked up, and what he saw caused an involuntary gasp. Right above them, on the edge, was the bear's hind paw. At the same instant, the whole grizzly started tumbling toward them! ... Dusty's reflexes took over at that point. With everything he had left, he pushed to the side with his legs, just as the plummeting bear went roaring by. It hit the ledge that had saved Aura Lee's life with a mighty thud, but his enormous weight demolished the small outcropping, and he continued his headlong fall to death.

Dusty's adrenaline going wild, gave him the added strength he needed to pull him and Aura

Lee up and over the edge. Laying there on the narrow trail, completely played out, they didn't move. Dusty looked at Aura Lee's dirty, tear streaked face and thanked the Lord once again for his divine protection.

Rising to his knees he scrutinized the area. Blood was everywhere, along with big hunks of bear fur. When his gaze fell on Shadow Spirit's still, blood splattered body, his heart skipped a beat and a lump came in his throat. "Oh' no!" He cried out, lurching to his feet.

Reaching her side, he dropped to his knees and gently lifted her big head into his lap. "Shadow ... Shadow Spirit," he said tenderly. "Yah gotta be all right ... There are a lot more trails we haven't traveled, or sunsets we ain't seen yet." Closing his eyes to hold back the tears Dusty didn't see the great wolf-dog's eyes flutter open.

"Dusty!" Aura Lee cried out with joy, "She's alive! ... Look, look, her eyes are open!"

Through tear blurred eyes, Dusty looked down at his brave-hearted companion. She looked a mess, her beautiful white coat was covered with blood, but as Dusty checked her over he found only a few wounds. It became obvious to him that most of the blood was grizzly.

As best as he could figure, the battle was a rip, roaring, one of a kind. In the final moments of it, Shadow Spirit must have had a painful hold on the griz and when he finally threw her off, she hit her head, and was knocked out. Fortunately for her ... and them, the bear was disorientated and took a step in the wrong direction and fell to his demise.

"Well girl, yah ready ta hit the trail?" He asked Shadow Spirit and then turning to Aura Lee, "How 'bout you?... Yah up ta coverin' more ground?"

"We can't get to Wrangell sitting here!" She answered, adding, "let's light shuck!" and they both burst out laughing at her attempt to talk like Dusty.

∾ CHAPTER 12 ∾

Even with Aura Lee's fall and the close call with the griz, Dusty and Aura Lee managed to make it to the high mountain valley, that had been their goal for the day. The ice on the small lake[13] had already given way to the warmer spring days. Snow, making this route impassable in subzero winter, was almost nonexistent, with the only exception being the deep shaded areas where the direct sun couldn't reach.

Dusty picked a campsite overlooking a picturesque lake and valley. He dug out fish hooks and line, told Aura Lee where to find bait and then asked her to go down to the lake to catch dinner. This way he knew she would take it easy and yet feel useful. By the time Dusty had the camp set up and a cook fire going, Aura Lee had caught four beautiful rainbow trout, not one weighing less than two pounds.

Dusty cut four willow limbs, about a half inch in diameter and three feet long. After cleaning and seasoning the fish, he secured each one on a willow, and propped them over the fire to broil. Aura Lee was impressed by Dusty's cooking. He was mighty tender to her too. He wouldn't let her lift a finger to help with the supper preparation, or the cleanup afterward.

The next day they decided to spend another day resting in the majestic splendor and solitude of this magnificent valley. As the day went by they roamed the different game trails around the lake. Dusty showed Aura Lee some of the edible plants and roots, growing in abundance in the wilderness. The day ended too soon for their liking. As they snuggled under their blankets, mother nature gave them one last display of her awesome beauty—the Aurora Borealis—they drifted off to sleep while the lights shimmered.

The next four days went by uneventful. On the fifth day they reached Skilak lake and camped where a small creek[14] emptied into it.

Dusty decided to build a raft and travel the length of the lake and then raft down the

Kenai River, where it exists the lake. It took Dusty almost a week to gather the materials and build the raft.

On the day Dusty finished building it, an old prospector/explorer named Dickey[15] came paddling up the lake in a canoe. Upon seeing smoke from their fire, he came ashore and enjoyed Dusty's and Aura Lee's hospitality. While on the trail, contact with other humans was rare and the opportunity to share news with one another was an occasion to savor. Over steaming cups of hot coffee, they listened to news he had picked up at the trading post in Kenai.

He told them of the parts of the river that could be dangerous on their way down, and to watch out for bushwhackers that were holding people up traveling the river. They spent most of the day in conversation. After supper Dusty invited Dickey to spend the night in their camp. He accepted.

At first light, when Dusty rolled out of his blankets, Dickey was long gone.

≈≈≈

After breakfast it didn't take long to pack up and load their belongings on the raft. When Dusty called Shadow Spirit and tried to get her on the raft, she would have nothing to do with it. Finally, giving up, Dusty told her to follow by land as best she could.

Dusty, with forethought, had rigged a makeshift sail out of a blanket. With a good breeze pushing them along, it was no time before the mouth of the river came into view. As they approached the outlet he dropped the sail and as Aura Lee folded it up, he unlashed the mast and casting it adrift, he picked up the pole he had made for navigating the river.

Around mid-afternoon they came upon the first serious set of rapids. However, long before these treacherous rapids came into view, the low, heavy rolling sound of their danger was audible. Both Dusty and Aura Lee were apprehensive about entering them and when Dusty guided the raft toward shore he could see relief fill Aura Lee's face.

He decided to have a look before starting down this first set. Securing the raft in quiet water, Dusty and Aura Lee followed the river down stream. The sounds of rapids were worse than the reality of them, and the channel looked wide and deep enough to allow the raft through without much danger.

Returning to the raft, the couple ate a late lunch

and then pushed off into the fast moving current and headed for their first experience through white water. As the raft picked up speed Dusty shouted, "Hang on!... This is gonna be one rip roarin' ride!"

Aura Lee saw his lips moving, but his voice was lost in the sound of the churning, crashing water swirling about them. Dusty didn't need to worry about Aura Lee hanging on. The minute she saw the rapids close up and personal, she grabbed a piece of rope and tied herself to the raft. The rapids were much worse than they looked from the shore. As the raft careened down river, being tossed about like a cork, Dusty gave up trying to steer it. Instead, he used his pole to push away from rocks. A direct hit on one of these could easily shatter their raft.

With a sudden lurch the raft breached the river, and before Dusty could do anything about it, the down stream side of the raft got caught under churning water and became violently tipped on its side. Dusty felt himself flying through the air and in the next moment, with a splash, found himself being pulled under by the raging river. With his lungs about to burst he fought for the surface. Which way that was, Dusty wasn't sure.

The current had a hold of him and tossed him

about like a twig. When his head broke the surface he gasped for air and got immediately slammed against a huge rock. Dazed, the river pulled him under again.

Aura Lee screamed when she saw Dusty get thrown into the river. There was nothing she could do. In less than a heartbeat, he disappeared. She thought she saw him come up once, but then a huge rock blocked her view. The raft rounded a bend, leaving behind the white water and any hope of seeing Dusty.

At this point the river widened and became very docile. Aura Lee had to stop the raft and this was as good a spot as any to try. With rope in hand, feet first, she jumped off the raft, and found the water barely knee deep. Wading ashore with the raft in tow, she quickly secured it to a nearby tree and headed up river.

She hadn't gone two hundred yards when a noise caused her to freeze in her tracks. She hadn't thought about the dangers that might be lurking in the woods when she left Dusty's Hawkens on the raft. Now as the thought occurred to her, it was too late. Swallowing hard she held her ground as the sound came closer.

"Well, what ever or who ever you are, come on out and show yourself!" she yelled at the approaching noise. On that command, to her relief, out bound Shadow Spirit, with tail wagging. "Oh Shadow Spirit," she cried, sobbing and holding the great wolf-dog close. "You were wise to follow us on land instead of going on that raft. ... Dusty's gone! ... Come on girl ... find Dusty ... find him, Shadow Spirit. I know you can."

As she pleaded, the great animal could sense Aura Lee's urgency. Without waiting for further command, she turned and bound up the river, with Aura Lee close behind. They hadn't gone far, when up ahead, Shadow Spirit came to a sliding halt on the river bank and danced around, excitedly barking. When Aura Lee caught up to Shadow Spirit, her fears became reality. There laying, half in the water, on the muddy river bank, was Dusty.

His face had a terrible bruise down the side and from where she stood, it didn't look as if he was breathing. Rushing to him, she calmly called his name, "Dusty" ... nothing. "Dusty. Please answer me!" She pleaded.

Reaching down, she took his arms and tried to pull him further up the bank. On the first tug, water came gushing from Dusty's mouth and then a choking cough, accompanied by a groan. With much effort, Aura Lee rolled him on his side and more water came pouring out, followed by more coughing.

"Wha ... what happened?" Dusty asked feebly. "I feel like a herd of caribou ran through the middle a me! There ain't a part a me that didn't get stepped on." Reaching up he touched his face and wrenched with pain. "Doggone! Now I remember. Well ...I kinda remember! That ole raft pert near turned over and when it went up, I shor' nuff went fer a swim. I shoulda faller'd your lead and tied myself on. I'll know better next time!"

"Next time?" Aura Lee asked, with disbelief in her voice. "You're not getting back on that... that raft!" She said, more as a statement than a question.

"Why shor' I am! It's like gettin' throwed from a hoss, if'in yah don't get back on, ya'll be a feared of it the rest of your life." Dusty didn't wait for any more questions. He got wobbly to his feet and headed down river.

The rest of the day they spent drying out their gear and making repairs on the raft. Dusty was in obvious pain, but never once said a thing about it. It was a forgone conclusion in the wilderness, unless you were completely incapacitated, you kept moving.

Shadow Spirit stayed by Dusty's side until he and Aura Lee boarded the raft the next morning. Again she refused to ride the river.

With the new pole Dusty had cut, he pushed off and headed into the main current. The river, at this point widened out and meandered lazily through awesome canyons and dense evergreen forests. From time to time, an eagle swooped down on the river with his razor sharp talons, and with perfect timing, would pluck an unsuspecting fish from the river.

A variety of wildlife was in abundance, from the smallest creature to a ferocious grizzly. When the big bruin lumbered out of the woods, it took Dusty and Aura Lee by surprise, and for a moment they thought it might come after them. Much to their relief, the bear only gave them a casual glance, then he went about the business of digging grubs from under a rotten log.

The slow moving current and warm sun, made for a comfortable day as they floated down the river. By nightfall the couple was close to the confluence of the Russian and Kenai River. It was then that Dusty smelled wood smoke, and as they rounded a bend, a small Indian village came into view.

Dusty was apprehensive as the current pushed

them toward the village and the excited, waiting Indians.

As the raft bumped the bank, the Indians swarmed around them, terrifying the wits out of Aura Lee. Dusty took hold of her hand and gave it a reassuring squeeze. The Indians began closing around them even tighter, with menacing looks on their weathered faces. Dusty didn't blink or back up. When the Indians became completely silent, he knew whatever was going to happen, it was about to take place, and how he handled it, could mean the difference between life and death.

Dusty knew not to show fear, as a tall, resplendent Indian stepped forward. His commanding presence left no doubt in Dusty's mind ... this was the man in charge. Dusty also knew that a man's eyes say a lot about him, that they truly are the windows to his soul. When their eyes met, he could see strong determination, as well as kindness in them. They were the color of cold, gray steel, but the smile lines around them softened and gave the impression that he was inwardly smiling at Dusty.

Ever so slowly Dusty let a smile come to his lips and in return the Indian started smiling too. In that instant the tension disappeared and everyone started talking at once.

To Dusty and Aura Lee's surprise, several of the natives could speak English, and in no time they were sitting around the campfire sharing information about the river. The chief told them, that less than one sleep away, the river became very treacherous and that it would be impossible for the raft to pass over it. He offered the use of one of their skin covered river boats and said when they reached Kenai, they could leave it at the trading post and one of his men would pick it up later.

⧯⧯⧯

The next morning, Shadow Spirit gave the Indians quite a start as she came charging into camp. If it wasn't for Dusty's quick reflexes, one of the natives would have taken a shot at her, but Dusty saw what was happening and in an instant put himself between the wolf-dog and the surprised native. After Dusty explained about Shadow Spirit, the morning returned to normal and the couple prepared to leave.

The skin covered boat was a definite change for the better. It maneuvered surprisingly easy and it was quite sturdy. When they approached the rapids the Indians had told them about, Dusty's stomach started to knot up. With his near drowning still fresh on his mind he wasn't sure he wanted to deal with this white water. He thought maybe it would be easier to portage around it, but down deep inside he knew he was deceiving himself. For the first time in his life, he felt real fear, and if he didn't face it head on, it would be with him the rest of his life. After coming to grip with this, he swallowed hard, pointed the boat into the main channel, and with a shout, they shot down the river.

At the trading post in Kenai, Dusty and Aura Lee met Captain Swanson.[16] He was the owner of the trading post. After explaining about the boat the Indians loaned them, Dusty asked about a ship sailing south. To their disappointment they had just missed the L. J. Perry, under the command of Cap Lathrop. She had sailed on the morning tide, and was the last ship expected until the end of the month.

With this news, the only other choices they had were by foot or horseback, so they headed for the stable at the end of town. There, with any luck, they would find horses they could buy and continue their journey to Homer ... on their trail to Wrangell.

⇜ CHAPTER 13 ⇝

After securing two saddle horses and one pack animal, Dusty and Aura Lee found the two story building made of rough cut lumber and logs that passed for the town's only hotel. The rooms were small and sparsely furnished: a bed, a dresser, and a washstand with a basin and a pitcher of water sitting on it.

Dusty surprised Aura Lee by having a large copper bath tub brought to their room. After the deskclerk made several trips to the kitchen, it was filled with hot water and lots of soapy bubbles. This was a luxury not often afforded a lady on the Alaska frontier, so she took full advantage of it while she could and soaked in it for an hour.

After a long bath and a restful nap, supper was in order, so Dusty and Aura Lee went looking for a place to eat.

Not far from the hotel they spotted a sign on the front of a tent that read: Beef Steak Dinner with Fried Taters and Hot Apple Pie~ 4 Bits~ (Coffee Extre) The words "Beef Steak" were all Dusty needed to read.

"Shucks!" Dusty exclaimed, "I ain't had me a beef steak since a leavin' Seattle … come on darlin', let's go wrap ourselves around a couple of them there steaks 'afore headin' south." It was hard for Dusty to believe they had real beef in Alaska, but when they got inside, sure enough, it was real beef.

The grub tent owner, a jovial, rotund gent said, "Some of the original Russians that settled the area brought cattle with them from Russia. When Russia sold the Territory and pulled out, some of them decided to stay on and raise cattle. The only thing is, because of all the interbreeding, the cattle are getting smaller. That's why I have ta charge so much for a steak."

What ever the reason for the price of the steak, it didn't matter to Dusty, as soon as he took the first bite, he forgot all about the cost.

Dusty and Aura Lee woke to a drizzly, gray morning and found the temperatures had dropped dramatically. After a hardy breakfast of fried ham, eggs and potatoes, and scalding hot coffee to wash it down, he and Aura Lee headed for the livery stable.

As the two walked down the boardwalk, Shadow Spirit appeared from nowhere, barking and wagging her tail in an excited greeting. "Where yah been hidin'? " Dusty asked as he reached to pet the great wolf-dog's head. He knew Shadow Spirit probably slept in the woods outside town. She didn't like town or strangers, so when they got close she slipped away. How she knew they were headed down the trail was a mystery to Dusty, but then again, she was always doing uncanny things.

Even though the day was gloomy and gray, the couple had a grand time. The well-marked trail made travel easy and the miles went by quickly. The horses were trail wise, and had an easy gate. To Dusty's surprise and pleasure, Aura Lee was a fine horsewoman. By supper time they had covered half the distance to Kachemak Bay. Without a doubt they would reach their destination sometime tomorrow in late afternoon.

◦◦◦

The next morning, Shadow Spirit, with an impatient bark, let Dusty and Aura Lee know she was ready to hit the trail. The sky was an azure blue and promised to bring a picture perfect day for travel. In no time they were overlooking Kachemak (Kach' uh mak) Bay and the small settlement of Homer.

It wasn't hard to find Mrs. Banks' gallery on the Spit, and when they arrived, she had good news for them. She told them that just yesterday, with the help of Mr. Smith, Captain O'Brien was moved back to his boat. This meant that the Captain was on the mend and the life threatening danger was past. After thanking Mrs. Banks, the couple, with Shadow Spirit by their side, headed down the Spit to find the Utopia..

The boat, tied up at the dock, looked all but abandoned. As they approached, Dusty, in an attempt to attract someone's attention, yelled out, "Yo. On board the Utopia!"

After a moment, a tall, thin, dark haired man, wearing a black frock coat, stepped from the captain's cabin and introduced himself as Mr. Smith. He said he had been attending Captain O'Brien through his recovery and then invited Dusty and Aura Lee on board.

The Captain greeted them with a big smile and a congratulation on their marriage. His pale skin color gave away his charade of well being. When he said he was ordering the Utopia to get underway tomorrow on the morning tide for Seattle his voice was weak and didn't have its normal crispness.

"Are yah sure yer ready ta make the voyage?" Dusty asked, with concern in his voice.

"Of course I am!" Answered the Captain with some of the old fire in his voice, and to emphasize that the subject was closed, he asked Mr. Smith to have the crew assemble on main deck at noon. The Captain said he needed to rest so Mr. Smith showed Dusty and Aura Lee to their quarters below deck.

At noon with the help of Mr. Smith, the Captain, weakly made his way to the main deck to address his crew. He told them to make ready to get under way on the morning tide. The crew showed their malcontent with this order, by mumbling among themselves. If the captain could have seen the devious looks they gave each other he would not have returned to his bunk trusting his orders would be carried out.

The next morning Dusty and Aura Lee slept in. When they awoke they were surprised to find the boat still tied to the dock. Sensing something was wrong, Dusty quickly dressed and told Aura Lee to lock the door behind him and stay in the cabin. Grabbing his Hawkens and checking the load, he headed for the Captain's cabin. On deck he ran into Mr. Smith, who was also heading for the Captain's cabin with a great deal of concern on his face.

After knocking several times and receiving no answer ... they opened the door and walked in. Upon hearing the door open, Captain O'Brien woke with a start. "What's goin' on. Why ain't we movin?" he yelled, "This is mutiny! Mr. Smith," he said in a calm voice. "May I borrow those pearl handle Colts you keep under your coat?"

"Of course, but what will I use?" Mr. Smith asked ... "Dusty and I intend to back you, but not empty handed."

"Over there in the cabinet, next to my desk, you'll find a twelve gauge shotgun. The shape I'm in, I couldn't handle it ... but I'm sure you can." Lurching to his feet, the Captain headed to the main deck with Dusty and Mr. Smith close behind.

As the trio approached the ladder leading to the main deck, a form appeared at the end of the passageway. In the blink of an eye, the Captain had one of the pearl handled Colts out and leveled at the man he recognized as the first mate. "Hey!" He shouted at the man. "Turn around real slow you son of a sea urchin or by thunder, I'll blow yah into the next life!"

The man slowly turned, the fear on his face unmistakable. He started to speak but the Captain interrupted with a harsh, "Shut up! ... I'll do the talkin'. If you don't get this boat underway immediately, I'll hang you or anyone else from the yardarm ...Is that clear?"

"Ye ... Yes sir!" he stuttered.

"Now git!" the Captain ordered in a commanding voice. The first mate turned and literally ran up the ladder in relief and fear for his life. He knew now he had misjudged the Captain's illness in his attempt to take over the Utopia.

It was slack tide when the Utopia slipped away from her berth in Kachemak Bay. The tension on board was so thick you could cut it with a knife and the first mate could look no one in the eye.

Aura Lee stood at the rail drinking in the surrounding beauty of the picturesque bay as the Utopia glided over the calm, azure blue waters. The great white wolf-dog sat at her feet and when she jumped and began to bark and wag her tail excitedly, Aura Lee turned and looked in the direction that had Shadow Spirit's attention. She broke out in joyous laughter and patted the wolf-dog on the head saying, "Oh' Shadow Spirit, you can't go play with that cute little sea otter. If you jumped in the water you'd scare the poor little thing to death … and besides he can swim better than you!" Aura Lee laughed again and reached down and playfully ruffled Shadow Spirit's soft, white coat.

The days on board the Utopia were blissful and serene. The weather couldn't have been more perfect. Evenings found Aura Lee and Dusty strolling the deck, hand in hand or just sitting by the rail with Shadow Spirit by their side, watching the night sky aglow with the light of a billion stars.

Even Captain O'Brien seemed better. Being at sea was like medicine to him, and every day his strength increased. On the final day of the voyage he appeared to be his old commanding self, right down to his freshly brushed uniform and the jaunty tilt to his sea captain's cap. He announced, "We will be making port in two hours. Prepare to disembark." He pointed to some ominous clouds building over the snow covered mountains to the east. He said a storm was blowing in. He could feel it on the freshening wind. Wrangell seemed peaceful enough, the dock area was buzzing with men loading another steamboat called, The City of Seattle, with bales of furs that would eventually be made into fashionable coats for wealthy Easterners and Europeans.

As Aura Lee stepped down the gangplank, the men on the dock stopped their work. A few made off-color remarks and Dusty fixed them with a mean look that made them turn away. Dusty had a bad feeling about this place and wished they hadn't decided to stay over a day or two before going on to Skagway. Even Shadow Spirit walked with her hackles up and her senses on full alert.

If Dusty would have known what Wrangell, the town some said was worse than any lawless town in the Old West, was like, they would have never stepped foot off the Utopia.

CHAPTER 14

It had been sometime since Dusty had been in a town that had all the earmarks of trouble, but this one had them all—and more. Between the dock and the hotel, Dusty and Aura Lee saw four fist fights and thought they were going to be in the middle of a gun fight, when two hard cases came flying out of one of the many saloons along the main street.

The only thing stopping the two from grabbing iron was a tall, thin man with a sweeping bushy mustache. He was wearing a flat crowned, black hat and frock coat. In an instant, he stepped up to one of them and busted the unsuspecting man over the head with his six-gun, that seemed to just appear in his hand.

The man was unmistakably the law, he had a

marshal's badge on his vest and it was obvious he knew what he was about, but there was something else … something that was familiar to Dusty.

❦

The hotel was a typical frontier hotel … adequate at best. The only redeeming thing about it was the small, but clean restaurant, located in the lobby.

As the couple entered, the aroma of the food increased Dusty's appetite two fold. "I'm as hungry as bear," he said, "I sure do hope they have plenty of grub back there in that kitchen."

"I'm sure they do darling." Aura Lee said sweetly with a smile on her lips.

Dusty loved her smile and it always made his heart skip a beat, just as it did the first time he saw it on her beautiful face. He put his buckskin clad arm around her shoulders and guided her to a table on the far side of the room. After sitting her so she could look out the window, Dusty put himself with his back against the wall so he was facing the door. He slowly slipped his colt from the holster, so no one would notice, and laid it carefully beside him on the bench. He didn't much like the feel of this town and he wasn't going to take any chances.

The waitress confirmed Aura Lee's beautiful but sensitive nose when she said the supper special was beefstew and fresh baked bread. It sounded good to both of them so Dusty ordered three portions, two for himself and one for Aura Lee.

As the waitress left to place their order, the marshal, who had stopped the gunfight earlier, stepped through the door. He stood there a moment and surveyed the room. His eyes missed nothing and when they met Dusty's, a flicker of recognition came to them. It was at that instant that Dusty remembered who he was and where he had known the marshal.

A smile of recognition came over the marshal's face, and he quickly crossed the dining room and was standing in front of their table reaching to shake Dusty's hand and saying, "Why Dusty ... Dusty T ..."

Dusty sprang to his feet interrupting the marshal, "Sourdough!" He said a little too loud, "Dusty Sourdough." Shaking the marshal's hand he noticed everyone in the restaurant was watching them, so he quietly asked the marshal to join them. "Marshal I'd like yah ta meet my wife, Aura Lee."

"It's a pleasure to meet you marshal," she said.

"The pleasures all mine ma'am, but my friends call me Wyatt"

"This is the famous Wyatt Earp," Dusty said to Aura Lee. "We did some marshalin' together back in Dodge City a long time ago." For a brief moment Dusty's mind drifted back to those rough and tumble days of yesteryear when young men knew no fear.

"Well" said Wyatt, "yah finally settled down and found yourself a wife, and a right pretty one too. I never thought you'd find a woman that would put up with your cantankerous ways." The trio had a good laugh at Wyatt's comment. Then Dusty invited the marshal to dine with them and he graciously accepted.

The conversation over supper was congenial and filled with old times. Over hot apple pie the talk turned to the present and as Dusty and Aura Lee said their goodbyes, Wyatt turned to Dusty and said with a serious tone to his voice, "Why don't you come by the office in the morning? Seein' how you're here in Wrangell, maybe I could get you to help me out?"

The next morning, before sunup, Dusty slid out of bed and lightly kissed Aura Lee on the cheek, trying not to wake her. He loved to watch her sleep and this morning was no different, but this morning he had something else to do. Strapping on his colt, he silently slipped out the door and down to the hotel lobby. The restaurant was open so he walked in, sat down and ordered a light breakfast of toast and a mug of steaming black coffee. Dusty noticed a couple of hard cases setting a few tables away. There was something familiar about them, but Dusty couldn't figure out just what.

When he got up to leave, the one who was facing him let his hand slip down to the butt of his tied down colt. Dusty didn't let on that he noticed the move, he paid his bill and left the restaurant never giving a second look to the two gunslingers who watched him with heightened interest.

"Mornin' Wyatt" Dusty greeted, as he stepped into the marshal's office. "What's the something yah wanted ta talk ta me about?"

"A couple hard cases came into town two days ago," Wyatt started. "Maybe you remember them? When we were marshalin' together back in Dodge City, you and I sent a pair of bank robbers to prison for twenty years, Curly West and Lefty Jackson. Remember Lefty had two boys? One about fourteen and the other around sixteen."

"Yah. ... how can I forget? Those boys were

trouble even back then, stealin' from the general store and beating up on the smaller boys. They ought ta be full growed by now."

"They are. ... and they're here in Wrangell!" Wyatt got up and went to a file cabinet, setting next to the one and only cell, and pulled out a wanted poster. When he handed it to Dusty, a look of recognition came over his face.

"Why, I seen these two polecats at breakfast, just afore I came here." Dusty declared. "The Jackson brothers, they turned out just like their pa ... no good. This here poster says their wanted fer horse stealin' down Texas way, that's a hangin' offense. Yah reckon they're a runnin' from the law or a huntin' you and me?"

Wyatt thought for a minute and then answered. "They have ta be runnin', there's no way they could know I was here. ... You didn't know you'd run into me and I for sure didn't know you were in Alaska, let alone Wrangell. ... No, they're runnin', we just happen ta be where they're a runnin' too."

Dusty and Wyatt discussed what their next move should be, and they both agreed that they should meet the situation head on. Wyatt strapped on his famous Buntline Special and Dusty checked the loads in his Colt. Both, with a look of determination on their faces, stepped out into the early morning darkness and started up the wagon-rutted street to meet their destiny.

Most of the town was still asleep as Dusty and Wyatt made their way toward the cafe. It was hard to believe that Wrangell was such a dangerous place. "But," Wyatt said, "it's rougher than Thombstone ever thought of being."

Dusty was pondering this and other things Wyatt told him when a shot rang out from between two buildings to the left of them. It was hard to say who pulled their six-gun faster, Dusty or Wyatt, but when they both fired it sounded like one thunderous shot. Then another shot came from the darkness of an alley further up the street but before Dusty or Wyatt could return fire, the most horrendous, blood curdling cry came from the alley darkness. They could hear the screams for help from a man obviously being attacked by some sort of wild animal.

Dusty threw a couple of shots in the direction where the first shot had come from and then sprinted toward the alley. By the time Dusty reached the alley all he could hear was a low guttural growl and the whimpering, begging voice of a man scared out of his wits. The man had managed to get himself to a temporary place of safety, perched precariously on top of some wooden crates. Standing below him, ears back, growling with teeth bared, was Shadow Spirit.

"Well, well," Dusty said, "looks like yah treed yourself a real polecat this time, and by the looks of his arm, he'll 'member you while he grows old in the gray-bar hotel."

Reaching up and jerking the dry gulcher off the crates, Dusty recognized him as one of the hard cases from the cafe. "I guess yah went from horse stealin' ta dry gulchin'. Well son, you've reached the end of the line. You and your brother are going ta be in the calaboose a good long time."

At that moment Wyatt came down the alley with the other Jackson brother being pushed reluctantly along in front of him. Wyatt's prisoner was holding a bloody arm and protesting every step of the way. The marshal told Dusty that his last volley of shots must have found a target, because as Dusty entered the alley after the second shooter, the other polecat came stumbling out between the two buildings hollering he was shot and was giving up.

By the time Aura Lee got up and was down-stairs looking for Dusty, he and Wyatt were in the hotel cafe talking about old times over a cup of hot coffee. "Tomorrow," Dusty was saying, "Aura Lee and I will be heading for Skagway for a couple of days and then back ta Hope. We got plenty ta do afore winter sets in. What about you Wyatt, you fixin' ta keep marshalin' here in Wrangell?"

"No ... no, after this morning's ruckus I realized this is a young man's game and I'm not young anymore. This little town's as rough as any one I've ever been in, and rougher than most.

"When I took the job, it was on a temporary bases until they could find another marshal. I'll be headed back ta Seattle in the next few days."

When the two old friends said their goodbye's on the dock the following morning, there was a sadness in both their eyes. They were smiling and joking about seeing each other again, but they both knew the chances of that were pretty remote.

As the boat slipped away from the dock, the stately figure of a man with the glint of a marshal's badge on his chest could be seen walking away. His head was down, and if someone would have been watching, they would have seen him try to blink back a tear, that silently rolled down his weathered cheek.

⇔ CHAPTER 15 ⇔

The waters were alive with otters, seals, and even an occasional whale or two. The couple stood on deck and talked of the things they would see when they got to Skagway the next morning. When Aura Lee asked Dusty earlier about the goings on in Wrangell, he brushed it aside as if it was nothing. Aura Lee knew better, but she also knew it wouldn't do any good to go on about it.

The day was wonderful and warm and Cap Lathrop had invited them to dine at his table for the afternoon meal. While standing at the rail waiting for lunch to be served, a familiar face approached the couple.

"Why good afternoon Mr. Smith. I thought you left on the Utopia when she left for Seattle?"
"No," answered Mr. Smith, "I decided to stop in

Skagway and the Utopia was sailing straight through to Seattle. There was room on board the L. J. Perry so here I am. I heard rumors of a gold find in the Klondike and everyone headed that way would have to go through Skagway. Maybe I can figure out a way to make a living off them."

"Good luck Mr. Smith," Dusty said, shaking his friend's hand.

"It won't have anything to do with luck, you can bet on that!" Mr. Smith said with strong conviction. "Maybe we'll see each other again, I won't be hard to find, just ask around for Soapy ... Soapy Smith!"

Dusty and Aura Lee knew the time was drawing near that they would need to start for Hope. Already the sun was setting earlier each day and soon the leaves would be changing color and dropping to the ground.

Their honeymoon had been filled with enough adventure to last most people a lifetime, but for Dusty and Aura Lee it was just beginning. The adventures to come in their lives would be rewarding and never ending, after all ... they were on their road to destiny.

1 *The Adventures Of Dusty Sourdough: A Gift For Dusty.*
2 Johnny Dynamite O'Brien (1851-1931) Captain of the *Utopia*, brought the first settlers to Hope.
3
4 Now the town of Seward.
5
6 Athabascan Indian word meaning: one that walks with heels.
7 Charles Miller staked the first recorded claim on Resurrection creek.
8 Squaw candy: dried, smoked salmon with a sweet flavor.
9 Outside is an Alaskan term meaning anywhere beyond Alaska.
10 *The Adventures Of Dusty Sourdough: A Gift For Dusty.*
11 Aura Lee was a love song written during the Civil War by a soldier missing his Aura Lee.
12 The Cannon Ball was the name used frequently in the 1800s for the Turnagain Arm because of its vicious bore tides.
13 This lake was later named Juneau Lake.
14 This small creek was later named Hidden Creek.
15 W.A. Dickey gave Denali the name Mt. McKinley in 1897 in honor of President McKinley.
16 Captain Swanson in the 1880s owned a schooner, the trading post in Kenai, and was the man who grubstaked Alexander King, who was the first American to discover gold in Alaska.

THE ALASKA WILDERNESS SERIES

VISA   **Please ship the following to:**   **MasterCard**

First Name _____ Last Name _____

Mailing Address _____

City _____ State _____ Zip _____

Phone Number _____ Fax Number _____

❏Check ❏Money Order ❏VISA ❏M/C

Credit Card Number _____

Expiration Date _____ Signature _____

	Quantity	Total
A Gift for Dusty—Book 1 (Twelfth Edition) 6.95 ea.	_____	$ _____
Trail to Wrangell—Book 2 (Fourth Edition) 9.95 ea.	_____	$ _____
Adventure Gold—Book 3 (Fourth Edition) 9.95 ea.	_____	$ _____
Adventure Fire—Book 4 (Second Edition) 9.95 ea.	_____	$ _____
Trail's End—Book 5 (First Edition) 9.95 ea.	_____	$ _____
Alaska's Dusty Sourdough Memories by Request—Music CD (11 Songs) 12.95 ea.	_____	$ _____

Kindly add $3.85 for first item for Shipping and Handling. $ _____
$1 per each additional item.

Grand Total $ _____

Please send orders to:

OLD ALASKA TODAY PUBLISHING

HC 33, Box 3191
Wasilla, Alaska 99654-9723

Orders shipped via Priority Mail. Allow 10 days for delivery.

www.dustysourdough.com